I0768866

Nathan Dragon's THE CHAMP IS HERE will burrow inside the muck and marrow of your life like all good writing should. These flash fictions cut like an X-Acto knife into thick cardboard, leaving behind beautiful and weird shapes that will read like a Rorshack test for the discerning reader.

-Robert Lopez, author of *Asunder, A Better Class of People, Dispatches from Puerto Nowhere*

Nathan Dragon's writing illuminates the fog between words and things, intensifying our desire to see and understand both the fog and what lies beyond it. Saussure writes, "Without language, thought is a vague, uncharted nebula." Dragon writes, "I've always wanted to build a lighthouse, so I am here." THE CHAMP IS HERE serves as a beacon, charting a course by which the relation between thought and language is revealed as no less vague than radiant.

-Evan Lavender Smith, author of *From Old Notebooks* and *Avatar*

Nathan Dragon's miniature worlds of domesticity are sharp and voice-driven, with the compression of Diane Williams and the whimsy of Robert Walser stories. They are full of sublime beauty and longing, wringing your heart and reminding you what it means to be alive.

-Babak Lakghomi, author of *Floating Notes* and *South*

People staring at themselves like the old man at the gas station stares at the gambling machine. Never losing isn't the same as winning. "The short and long life of a one liner." Nathan's characters in THE CHAMP IS HERE are trying to be ok with what's already there.

-Jake Lenderman, musician, MJ Lenderman and Wednesday

Nathan Dragon has written some of my favorite contemporary American stories.

> -Kathryn Scanlan, author of *Aug 9 - Fog, The Dominant Animal, Kick the Latch*

From a distance, these seem like gentle stories about men who live ordinary lives in quiet towns. But come closer, and you will find anger, jealousy, paranoia, and a longing for beauty so vivid and fierce that it escapes language. Nathan Dragon is the master of the deceptively simple sentence.

> -Merve Emre, contributing writer at The *New Yorker*

I loved THE CHAMP IS HERE, and found myself reading many of the stories out loud just to hear how the words glow. The stories are like postcards from a town contained within a glacier—far off and so wonderful that you grow wild to get as close as you can.

> -Nicolette Polek, author of *Imaginary Museums* and *Bitter Water Opera*

THE CHAMP IS HERE

stories
Nathan Dragon

Cash4Gold Books LLC
New York, USA

1st Edition, 2024
Type + design by Raegan Bird

Copyright © Nathan Dragon, 2024

CONTENTS

THE CHAMP IS HERE

NATHAN DRAGON

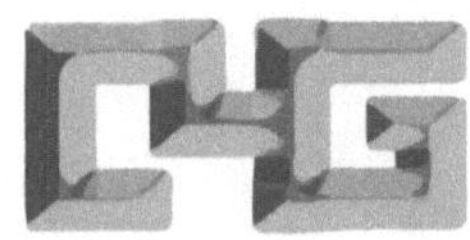

Cash 4 Gold Books

The things that were real to other people weren't real to me, but the things that were real to me, they... yes they still are.

- *The Recognitions,* William Gaddis

Like a champ I have got a record,
I'm knockin' out the frauds in a second

- Boogie Down Productions, "My Philosophy"

You see a curtain move in the wind, you can bet I'm betting against you again.

- Silver Jews, "How to Rent a Room"

THE CHAMP IS HERE

THE CHAMP IS HERE

He'd never seen one of those before, one of the classic ones like in the cartoons.

In real life, though, it was pretty big and ugly in a pre-historicway, and scaly.

A classic woodpecker.

He saw it one day when he pulled into the driveway, caught a quick glimpse of some red and black bobbing its way up the tree then out of sight into branches and glare.

There was a pile of bark and wood chips at the foot of the big old scraggly pine and there were holes in a haphaz-ard almost-pattern going up the trunk.

Man, he thought, a classic woodpecker.

He wanted to tell someone right away and badly.

Show them the piles underneath the tree he parked in

front of every day.

Man, he thought, like the cartoon. Never seen one like that before. Never seen a classic woodpecker in real life. Not once in his life.

He'd seen a different kind once—stiff-dead on its back in the weeds for a few days, legs sticking up out of the bentgrass. Didn't look real anymore. Half-taxidermic traces. Familiarity just shy of being able to tell how it reminded him—like the lotion smell that reminded him of music instead of the fruit it says it smelled like.

He felt like he learned something when he saw this real-life classic woodpecker. Like something out of a nature program. A shot of him pulling into his driveway and seeing the woodpecker through the windshield—there it was, right there in plain view.

He'd see it as soon as he turned onto his street because he started to look for it and his house was the first house on his street and the tree was right by the driveway.

And when he'd see it, he'd slow the car down, drive softly, and stop to watch it. Best seat in the world.

He took pride that this woodpecker, a Pileated woodpecker—he'd done his research—chose the pine tree in front of his house and not a tree in front of anyone else's house in town. This gave him something to come home to at the end of the day, look forward to: the woodpecker and the feeling.

Man, this was a future he could settle into.

A thing to be proud of.

When he stopped seeing it, when it stopped coming, he started looking out the back and side windows.

He'd had something special there. It'd even lifted his spirits. And even now, sometimes, when he thinks about the classic woodpecker, like how he hadn't heard it make a sound, it amazes him, how he'd never heard it pecking or whatever else it did.

But he did see it a last time: Its profile and the way it moved. Out the kitchen window, flying off somewhere, and he thought about boxers. How boxers could really take lessons from the classic Pileated woodpecker. With the way its head bobbed. How the bird seemed swifter than a featherweight, jabbing, moving.

Bob and weave.

Stick and move.

Nobody fights like that anymore, he'd said aloud, thinking about it and shaking his head.

When he stopped seeing it, at first he worried. Then he wondered where it went and he pictured himself fighting some homeowner somewhere in town, the homeowner that had the pine tree on their property that the woodpecker went to now.

Jab and move, baby.

Stick and move.

He'd knock on the door and spit and say, The Champ is here! He'd flutter his feet in complex footwork and throw a haymaker the moment his opponent looks down.

There had to have been something he could've done to have made it last or to make it come back and stay.

Maybe he should've parked up the street so not to bother it.

Anything he could've done so that it would've stayed. And not've gone to somebody else's pine tree.

Most things were like that. How it always happened, happened before and would happen again.

Something to react to.

And most things.

BUD

This is what I mean, so I'm clear: I wipe the mirror, then I pass the razor over the stubble while I'm looking in the mirror, taking away the shaving cream from my face in little curved rectangles. Then I watch my skin underneath the last pull get pinkly irritated and the mirror fog up again.

I get into the shower and turn the water on—in that order. It's the touchiest faucet and it really has gotten my stomach scalding and I feel jealous of something. I put on some jeans and a navy T-shirt with a breast pocket and thin black cotton socks and my tan tennis shoes and I am cheering myself on the whole way—Keep going, bud! and, I'll help ya, bud!

I finish dressing by dressing like a pumpkin: I put on my orange sweater and forest green winter cap so that I will be nice and warm since my hair is wet, even though my skin is raw.

The last thought I have before I finish dressing is this: I need something to defend. A world record or something.

DAILY

He walks home daily, just thinking. Most of the time when he's thinking, he thinks of things like all the different names he might name a dog. Jacques would be fitting or maybe Sweet William, like a racehorse, like a flower.

He's always wanted a dog.

Something to give a meaningful name to.

Sometimes he goes out just to walk home and he wears layers. Layers are important, something that zips over something that buttons over something, crewnecks tucked in, hood and hat, depending.

Then he's cushioned in a situation that mainly has something to do with his biley stomach. He had to explain this to many people. But as soon as they ask why, he feels it welling up.

SPEAKING CANDIDLY

If it's rainy I spend the day inside, instead of outside on my lawn chair. If it's windy too, I can hear nuts and acorns raining down on the metal roof of the house. I often sense or see at least a speck of regret in the distance, visible though. A loon laughing through the wind, the squeak of branch on sheet metal.

On rainy days, sometimes, I go into town. It's usually so slow shopkeepers visit each other. They pop into the neighboring shop to say, How's it going? or, Ready for next month?—next month being the beginning of busy season.

A small tourist town.

Souvenir shops, sandwich shops, coffee shops.

A small grocery.

The pizza shop.

Sometimes you catch two, three, four shopkeepers speaking candidly with each other.

I want so badly to be let in on it. But they quiet up and go back to their shops whenever they hear the bell over their doors.

DISPLAY

When she gets home he'll have already done it.

It'll all be set up.

A least for the week, a fucking tableau.

He'll have something going on the stove too, for tonight.

He was quite proud of what he'd accomplished so far today. And the day's not over.

He talks to himself while pushing the cart about what it's like to be a proud hunter, or better, more like a predator—what a predator would do with its prey and lay it out like an offering to a mate. To be the type of provider he is. Just look-it.

He brings it home from the store, arranges it out all on the counter and kitchen table. All nice and very careful.

Look-it this, he thinks, a well-stocked pile of spoils. He sets up the display of what he managed to get. What he managed to bring back to the den.

A hunt's bounty.

All the gatherings and trappings caught in the chrome basket of the cart.

He'd even go as far as to think of himself and refers to himself as the Apex Pred. The way he moved around in the store. The way he procured a profusion of sustenance.

To think the most natural way. Impulse and instinct, the most biologically evolved for efficiency. But he doesn't know what that could mean to him—beyond some primordial tickling in his ears and hope for salvation from starvation for just one more day, and maybe even getting a nice tugging reward.

He'll get another list tomorrow morning when she leaves for work and the amount to cover it.

Another chance.

It's what he can do for her, however well, and however simple it looks. He doesn't think of it as less. He thinks: It's dangerous out there.

He hopes he can make the display tonight look appetizing, or at least okay, even seductive. He didn't want to push it too much. Subtly is sexy. That's why he went to the grocery store by himself in the mornings. He could spend the rest of the day laying it out, adjusting everything to make it look right because as he rearranges it all he'd eat from the pile, a snack here and there—just a couple of bites—pieces of fruit and lunch—some bread and some cheese. He has to try to make sure it doesn't look like he's eaten anything from it. Like he was patient and waited for her to get home from work and didn't cheat and he had control. Like as long as he wraps everything back up as it was, lock-baggy lock tracks lined up right with the deli sticker, bread bag twisted back up and tied up the way a machine would do it.

As long as the work he put into it is acknowledged.

JUICE

This morning, he pours some juice, walks to the table, sneezes, tries to stifle it and spills some juice. And again, a sneeze starts coming on. He tries to stifle it, spills, sneezes, tries to stifle it, spills. Now the cup's empty. Shit. Juice is kind of expensive. And this always happens.

IT'D BE NICE TO HAVE A SHARP-LOOKING COOLER

There was one week during this time when every day, on my way home, young blonde women with really long hair were driving extremely fast up the windy road in the opposite traffic, in medium-sized, white cars, non-stop, one and then another nearly floating over the yellow line.

Two times were very close calls.

I actually said, Yikes! to myself when it was happening.

They were all obviously different people driving different cars, but the similarity and speed of everything was startling.

When I told my wife about this experience, she shook her head. I started shaking my head along with her.

I did want to ask her if she thought they were all together somehow, and what kind of unit it could be. I mean they were flying! But I didn't say anything else and I am glad.

Then we went out to get some coffees, snacks, gallons of water, wipes, ice, a new cooler—as a little treat during this situation.

Why not? It's nice to have a sharp-looking cooler.

I picked the one that I thought I'd look best with at a cookout.

I wonder if my wife loves me enough.

WOODPECKER

The woodpecker used to be such a good thing. Something to look forward to, truly.

You could only get so mad over the damage, he thought. It was a woodpecker, after all.

Maybe would've even been good for the neighborhood, for whoever's peace of mind, could've described it as rustic, because of the nature.

There were plenty of things and sounds happening all the time that carried up the streets and alleys. It had been good to hear something from out of place. Only bothersome if the pecking was loud, close, and constant, by proximity. Not like ants or roaches crawling over all your shit, materializing out of nothing, on you, in everything needed.

Long after the fact, he found out it belonged to the

Flicker family. It was a Northern Flicker.

The woodpecking was the best sound he got to hear regularly. A non-people sound. Not any longer, though. Thanks to something people did do. And, come on, a jackhammer some street over. He saw them put the construction spray paint down.

And the woodpecker, dead in the sidewalk grass, on his way to the train.

It looked shiny, somehow impatient. The way a pair of empty shoes by the door looks like it holds a posture.

Whoever did it should've done it to the Big Shot and all the Big Wigs instead.

The ones who got paid to decide the things.

The only pure sound in the neighborhood muted by someone taking their rage out on the wrong thing. He blamed the ones who kicked the nature out to begin with, in the very, very first days.

Who could he trust now?

The woodpecker was probably poisoned. Pretty easy to get at any hardware store from pest control.

He felt like someone in the wrong place, headed somewhere worse.

The city was no good.

Too flat.

Too flat and now, no woodpeckers.

The morning after he saw it dead, he swore he could still hear it pecking down the street.

He put his shoes on and ran to check a few times. The trees were always empty. And then, there it was: hardly ruffled by the wind or sniffed out by a dog.

A dead woodpecker, a Northern Flicker, left in the grass. Then one day gone.

He noticed some sort of sense of control in the neighborhood started taking hold. A note on his neighbor's door that said: ENOUGH WITH THE PEANUTS!

Something must've happened at some point.

What would he watch from his window now?

LACUNAE

That this was the case for him.

On the couch.

Situated and it's got a nice ring to it: On the couch.

If he just sat with it long enough, it would come to him as something that was his, a little bit of himself.

He didn't ever know what anyone wanted him to say to them. Sometimes it was the fact that they had wanted him to say anything at all that had made him question it. He felt like he was expected to make a sound, so he said, What? real quick and breathy.

He could go through the list. He could stop and run through another one, a different list instead of or as well as or in addition to.

Perhaps compare the two.

Or he could think on it some more, for a while, lay out all of the pros, the cons of looking at the one versus the other.

Forget about going at it simultaneously. And forget about alternating.

For example: Here.

And here.

Or here.

And here.

Or one other one here.

Ahhh the thread between things.

Looking forward to a life spent staring into something then at something then through something. At least he could say he was looking, whether or not he was looking.

He saw that there were things around him: coffee cups or mugs, the desk, powders, a lighter pen wallet, some keys, clean clothes that have been folded and left on the chair under the window.

He was searching for the right word to use now. A word he'd read or heard on the radio or had rested his head on. He had to spell it out—costive—clearly for himself to see it, put that up against whatever he thought he'd heard. Or he had to sound it out, repeat it, and pit that against what he might've read.

Took a while.

Right?

And there was a long line when he arrived there. There was sleeping, thinking, eating, worrying, brooding, not thinking, being busy, forgetting and then forgetting what it is you forgot. It was something. Something was forgotten. He forgot something. He was standing in the entrance of a room.

Eventually, he sat down and crossed his arms, tapped

his fingers, rapped his knuckles. Wiped some residue from his hands onto his pants. What was he doing? He was doing something.

He got up and looked for things that could remind him: Graphite dust and ink squiggles inside a drawer, crumbs in the mayo, murals on the sides of the liquor stores across the street.

He knew of restaurants that still smelled of stale smoke thanks to the un-reupholstered furniture of the old smoking section. And when he listened, he heard a sound like tall pines squeaking or creaking in wind.

He felt like he had to keep looking.

Now it was nighttime, out of a window with the lights on. How it's all seeing in at that point. How if he wanted to see out he'd have to halve his hands in the shape of binoculars up to his face and pressed to the glass.

He felt his energies here were well spent.

He was always waiting to feel differently, an air of change, in order to begin. He was finally getting comfortable with it all.

Figuring out you just have to let it be or pick up and go with the way it is and the condition that it's in. Buy it as is. Houses and lead paint, layers of it chipping away: white, green, dark blue, white, white, white, yellow, off white, a minty green, copper-like and other things.

After a hard week, one end of a sweet gesture with someone and love. A treat. Chocolate ice cream at a drive thru. A little chance to get away. From one's own little life for a while. At least some weekend plans to get out of town, into a new state.

Based on what he thought people thought the world was like.

How he thought it would work out.

Something about people, something not about anyone.

Something, more, about a time of year and wrapping your mind around going north and heading downstream being the same thing.

PERSONALLY

Personally—of course, all of these are personal issues. Rotten fruit refusing to fall or some echoing threat like a baseball thrown at him, but it pings off a post, by that one angry kid or rough cousin growing up.

You're going to miss out on your entire life. Take a look around. You're living like birds dancing and a man describing the scene.

But how about all the floors he's ever lied down on? He's thankful for them. Like all the ceilings he's eased off under. Windows he's looked out from, porches sat out on. And outside resting in the grass supine, looking up.

Recently, but not recently enough, he was sick at home watching crime shows. He thanks God for those days.

A big brown owl plus snow a week later. The dog hesitating at the door in the cold. Deer jumping in the brush. Remember a sky of scratches like missing crystals from a chandelier?

This is a tourist town all the locals seem to be disappointed by, though they wouldn't ever admit it. The short and long life of a one-liner. He accidentally crosses a wet paint crosswalk and leaves a trail. *Sorry sorry sorry*, he thinks, I'm still out of plumb.

I AM A LITTLE WORLD

Sometime just after we moved here, on the tiniest Monday, it seemed like something new was low risk.

I started to take my coffee in a new way, with half-and-half and grade-A maple syrup. I wanted to change things up.

I think somebody said that maple syrup is brain food.

I used to take my coffee strong and plain, but today a golden rain falls in globs like applesauce.

And when it's warm and sunny we all love the ice cream they sell here.

I am thinking that I am the god of rising air, low pressure, fresh clouds, cyclical weather systems. I get strength from thinking this.

You ever feel like someone who you've seen around a lot but never met is a good friend?—or even someone you

fucking hate, like they've been messing with you?
   I am that one.

WORK THOUGHTS

He'd been cutting plastic decking, a small side job, when he thought: Jesus was a carpenter.

And also: Is this even carpentry if the wood is really plastic composite molded and grained to look like wood?

And another thing that caused him to stop a sec: when he realized he doesn't know what a terrace really is.

It's out on the terrace, someone might say.

If he was in that situation right now, he wouldn't know where to go or how to proceed.

Building the deck, worrying about how slippery the stairs will be. He'd leveled the newel, laid tread.

One thing at a time.

And no—that's all wrong, it was his dad that was the carpenter.

PET FENCES

A couple days ago, in the morning, pretty early, I got a phone call from what sounded like an older woman. She said, You put my electric pet fence in eighteen years ago and the other day some painters dropped a ladder and it severed the line. 13 Lynn Street, remember? If not, I have the paperwork.

She said she needed two more collars for two older cocker spaniels who are good, but still need the collars. It would make her feel better.

The phone number I have, my phone number for the last sixteen years at least, used to be this other guy's phone number—I guess he installed residential electric pet fences all around the North Shore. It also belonged to a guy named Bruce Adams at some point too. I get calls for Bruce and for

the electric pet fence guy—I forget his name—all the time.
His name might've been Bruce Adams too.
There are probably a lot of Bruce Adamses.

THE LADDER

When I was in my late twenties I was driving north, my panting dog in the back. At some point we moved over from 95 to some local street. But before that, with marshes below us, the highway elevated, and my mind was blown—a ladder stuck up from below, floating up just barely above the railing.

The top of a ladder, Vic! I yelled. Would you look at that!

I'd gotten hired onto another roofing crew earlier in the season. I liked the work. I'd had an eye for ladders. My mind, so warped by all the tinny work radios—classic rock and merengue, depending—said: Stairway to Heaven.

It wasn't though. Just 95-North into New Hampshire.

It was cloudless and hot that week. Easy to remember

that because I was always wet and heavy those days.

The ladder'd caught light in a way it shouldn't have. It blinded me—heaven! I was in heaven with my dog. I'd wanted to close my eyes and keep them closed. But I opened them because I had to. I wanted to live, and I wanted my dog to live too.

I'd never told anyone about that ladder because it seemed melodramatic and embarrassing at the time. Years later, though, when I thought of it, it made me feel hopeful. Someone who needed to escape did. Climbed up to the highway. Lived and kept living, and I kept driving. Kept living, too.

The only reason I opened my eyes was because my dog barked.

PARAKEET

Band I were visiting my folks for a few weeks.

One night, the elderly, somewhat understandably unstable neighbor called me around midnight. I missed the call and she left a message.

Can you come help me take the trash out? was how it started. Innocuous. Nothing.

But then she starts rambling, really rambling, Her message is over three minutes long, She ends the call with, Well if I can't even take the trash out, might as well kill myself.

So I'm like, Fuck, I can't have this. I immediately felt guilty and pictured the worst. I tried to call back right away.

No answer. FUCK.

I run down the stairs, across the street, up the stoop and I'm ringing the doorbell. Nothing.

I look in and I see the staircase's runner, the rug, askew down the steps, and I'm thinking: Uh-oh.

I run back home and knock on my parents' bedroom door like a child because I don't want to see a dead body. Plus, I half-think, in the moment, it's my fault for missing the call. Even if I was home all day, even if she should've called me earlier.

I'm telling my parents the whole thing—Joanie, next door, yada yada. My dad's snoring. My mom's sighing. My mom calls Joanie and Joanie picks up. You know you scared him half to death. You know he's always willing to help you. You've gotta tell him about the trash earlier. Maybe, I don't know... in the afternoon, she says.

My mom and I go over, do all the trash. I feel bad and like a child. But I can't look at dead bodies if I can help it—like at a wake or funeral. Not after seeing Pépère dead in the hospital the Easter he died.

A few years after that, I refused to go see his sister's Ta-tante's body in the funeral home when she died. They both used to watch me when I was a kid and my parents were working. I'd go downtown with Pépère or to Ta-tante's house. She was funny, and very afraid of birds. Maybe a year or two after Ta-tante stopped watching me regularly and only came over for a holiday party once where we had to hide our parakeet in the furnace room. She ended up seeing it anyway. Pépère, allegedly by accident, showed her the furnace room on a tour of the downstairs.

I don't think she'd ever been over because we'd moved and also there's always a reason, some rift or grudge in the Dragon family, so this all gets tangled up in my head.

A few days after the thing with my parents' neighbor's trash and the voicemail, I'm in the dining room with my mom talking about all this.

The shit with across the street and death and then Pépère and Ta-tante and hiding the parakeet.

When she goes on to tell me this beautiful story about a neighbor she had when she was a kid and lived in Castle Hill, a neighborhood in Salem.

She had this neighbor, Mr. Tardiff who bred parakeets.

And his wife, Mrs. Tardiff, Rita, decorated wedding cakes for people in the neighborhood.

Started his hobby with two abandoned birds and ended up caring for a flock of over 300 birds because people would bring him their parakeets to breed, and he'd get to keep an egg or two per clutch. Tardiff even developed, fine-tuned a new feed for his flock, a seed mix, that was supposed to be more healthy and wholesome.

I couldn't imagine so many people having parakeets in one town.

He had a swing in his yard that he let the neighborhood kids swing on whenever they pleased.

He'd show them all the parakeets. His basement was where they were all kept and bred.

It sounds like a classic premise to something horrible and sinister, but I guess he was really just a good guy, a nice neighbor. Mr. Rogers.

Listening to my mom explain this, I pictured a light mote coming angled in through the basement windows to the dirt floor, feathers floating in that dusty light. The chirping of all those birds, *Whos-a-pretty-Birdies*. Peaceful coos.

My mom's family got their birds from Tardiff.

My mom and dad had parakeets too, two of them before I was born, one when I was a real young child. All of them named after something that had to do with Elton John. Elton, or Benny, like "...and the Jets," or Levon, after another

Elton song.

A parakeet breeder and a wedding cake decorator—it seemed sweet.

I brought up another parakeet we got a couple years after my sister was born, but we didn't get it from the Tardiffs. I'm not sure why exactly. I didn't know them then and have only just become aware of them. We got the bird from a place called Curious Creatures. I remember this bird well. A blue one named Reggie—because, of course, Elton John's birth name was Reginald.

I remember asking my parents questions.

If the bird was lonely because it looked at itself in a little mirror all day.

If the bird knew that it was the reflection.

Why did this kind of bird live in a cage and not out with the seagulls and pigeons?

And why did they like Elton John so much?

It talked to itself a lot. We'd let it out and it would fly around the house. Doors and windows closed. Ceiling fans off so it wouldn't kill itself.

I didn't see when Reggie died. I was playing outside when it happened and it was hidden from me. He died, I think, of natural causes.

Because, later on, my mom'd told me she found him stiff and hanging upside-down from his wooden dowel perch.

Upside-down? I asked her.

And she said, Yeah, upside-down. Still holding on like a bat.

CRAIGS AND GREGS

Craigs are blondes.

Gregs are brunettes.

He thought of more and some felt great.

Mm...

Like standing outside in heavy fog, wearing a tee shirt. Gets damp and heavy. Wet and soaked, soaked through, sopping.

Craigs are sopping, he thought, and Gregs, having something to do with width, also have something to do with a smiley girth.

He thinks, It's going.

Guess what my name is?—he asked first chance he got. Just little ol' me?

WHATEVER IT IS

Everything that is said or that can be said about something, whatever it is, reduces it. That thing that is being
referred to, whatever was said about it—and even the rela-
tionship between that thing being spoken about or referred
to and whatever this thing is related to is reduced when
anything is said about any of it.

Something is or is-like some something specific, but
not only that.

Happens or doesn't; is whatever it isn't; skirting around
it.

It can be like a lot of things, like what it's made of, or
nothing related to it at all.

With that being said, there's probably more to it.

For example: The lake smells fresh like dirt and the

ocean smells like the ocean.

ocean smells like the ocean.

GROCERY STORES HAVE DIFFERENT NAMES, REGIONALLY

One time I sat in the shade and looked at a sunny patch on the surface of the lake—there was this rare hue of blue between the crests I knew at the time to exist only in one other place. Everything at my left—if I faced north—was just slightly out of reach.

In the Jewel-Osco, or Shaw's, or Albertsons. Food Lion, Hannaford's, Stop and Shop.

Driving along mountains, hills, plateaus, plains.

The ocean versus a lake.

A LIFE IN A SMALL HOUSE

He wore big special pants in those days. He remembers the delicious french fry store. He had big plans. But now he's thinking, I've gotten nothing done—he is thinking about a mediocre attempt at something maybe interesting.

He felt he was at an angle again. Couldn't give the feeling a name, just a handful of words—color-bound to an orange hue and slammed.

He feels embarrassed. Is he supposed to be embarrassed by this?

He wants a way of life. Something that originates with him.

He should try to keep himself busy. He should. Fingers at the top of his head pinching for one hair with texture and when he finds it, he softly pulls. Almost the perfect reverse of slurping a noodle.

He'll keep himself sitting down. Maybe open a private window.

He does have fun holding a grudge.

Justice and there were things to keep track of here. Ripley and Stacy Toole, those two.

IT'S COME TO THIS

After the PUSH on the door, there was no direction to follow.

We began to question how to act here, what to do—its being empty and our being the only customers. No one was here with B and me, although people wearing suits and going into buildings all the time were visible through the window.

I kept looking over at the matador stuck up there in the TV, still waiting for his bull.

B said she thought she saw the matador move.

The restaurant was still empty.

I looked at the door from the inside now. On this side of the door, I saw PULL.

Up on the Specials of the Day chalkboard I saw in large

letters:
    TRY OUR—
        ON THE HOOK TUNA TARTARE!
        SOFT SWEET-FRUIT SANGRIA!
        GET FUCKED FOIE GRAS!

LICKING THE SPOON

Their doubts never lined up like an overbite.

And it was a good thing; they were a buck luckier for it. That's how one of them said it, anyway. The other didn't know what it meant.

For being inside like they were, of a thing like they were.

Outside it sprinkled and puttered. It was leaking through the window mesh and onto the kitchen counter, glinting just right, a little flat up surface, gritting and fizzing in such a way that it all seemed un-outlined. And the air inside had a quality not unlike that of cloudy-daylight accented by the yellowing woods. It got ridiculous. To them, it felt like a nod. A wink.

Retirement dreams, baby, one said. It doesn't matter

which.

They fell in love and out of sleep, holding hands.

Whatever they had wanted this coming evening was going to come and they'd have to sit with it long enough because there wasn't much of a choice.

A decision needed to be made.

Gently.

So for once, no bother at all.

One of them didn't mention something that shouldn't have been mentioned to the other—a thing that can happen sometimes and is usually not too bad but can be. Ultimately a thing best left alone that sometimes isn't.

Better off not asking what. One of them thinking that other must have said something.

But.

Eh.

Let whatever's left be.

The point being that when something goes right through something else and settles, the thing as it is settles too.

When the one left and then returned to the room, each asked—at the same time—the other one to say something beautiful.

She asked, What's that even mean? She couldn't picture it. *Water breaking like teeth.*

And after when either one agreed with the other about anything, everything from there on was sweet.

Then they'd feel like doing something. That night. But something cheap.

Dandelion tea sat on the counter brewing in teak-light.

MAGNESIUM DREAMS

Magnesium feels good.

Magnesium in vegetable cellulose capsules in bottles from shelves in stores or from the mail.

Magnesium made from or up of amino acid chelate, citrate, and malate. "Chelate" to the best of my understanding—my regurgitation of a couple definitions—means a compound that has a molecule that will attach to a bigger metal atom at two points.

I get what those individual words mean. I can't picture it.

I suppose I don't understand all the reasons behind the mechanics.

I also read that chelated magnesium is something a body can easily absorb. Citrate as in citric acid. Malate, like salt of malic acid—this too, saying it like I get it.

I read the Supplements Facts on the bottle, then looked up those components to understand. I really don't.

It's been working though.

Taking the magnesium supplements.

For sleep.

I take the magnesium supplements for sleep.

I haven't been sleeping well since it got so quiet.

A YEAR IN THE FACE

Somewhere in Same Hues, June 6

A few books got stolen. By whom I'm not a hundred percent, though I have my suspicions. He was going to help us out on the next leg of the project.

Strange to be made paranoid by someone who claims to be paranoid.

I just had a thought that that seemed obvious—about the books. A book can be about anything. A book might also never be opened.

I was mostly angry all day, so I hid.

To Truth or Consequences, August 7

The to-do list has been growing since getting here. The pile of supplies growing with it—there's nowhere flat to put anything until we start using some things because we can make room to organize so we can work more efficiently.

I'm stepping away from our camp for the day to pick up a glass blower a few hundred miles away. He's been staying at a motel famous for its mineral baths.

We've been set up at the homestead about a month now. It's just a couple of recently fixed-up trailers behind a tomato greenhouse, all rented to us for the time being, by the farmer, until we finish building the house up the road or until he sells the trailers.

I like this trailer. I want to buy it after we move into the house, if we could think of how it could make sense. If we could cash in on the great metaphor.
I keep calling it that. But it means nothing.
There's no more room on any shore. I've always wanted to build a lighthouse, so I am here. In the desert, where at night it can feel like the shore.

I worked at the Gardens today some ways into town, before heading out in the early morning, in exchange for a nearly unused generator.

When I got back just a little while ago with the expert glass blower the cats were in the yard.
Certain pales of yellow and blue.

Today, it seemed, the desert had sucked in all sounds. And in town, everyone was walking around shielding their eyes from the sun, even in the shade, out of habit.

I feel the heat pull a drop of sweat from my chin. It disappears instantly into the paper.

Writing now I remember how having to skip lines when writing by hand a long time ago helped me think.

Gate's Pass, August 28

We needed to get a good view. Two hills. One across the gulch from the other. It could only peak out so much.

We're surveying. B's got all the equipment set up. I feel useless compared to her skills. She told me I could spot her.

When we first looked to come here, we rode horses down below where we are now. We'd been promised snakes but all we saw was a white-roofed mansion, where one of the West's most famous musician's had lived with his wife until she died. He still owns the house, but he's never been back.

We're, by some small chance, standing between a Key lime tree and a Meyer lemon tree twenty yards to each side of us.

Same Hues, August 29

I changed my handwriting up and when I looked at it I liked it. I wanted to keep it forever.

I debated if it was smart making a drastic change like that in the middle of a project that requires me to make so many notes. I thought maybe it could throw things off or on the other hand bring a much-needed freshness. Or maybe I could write in two handwritings so on paper it looks like a conversation's occurring.

A new way to hold the pen and everything. New to me at least. But my hand got sore and I let it go and went back to how I used to.

I slept in today to stay cuddled up. I know it's still a week away but B's going to the Midwest for a little. I'll have to work smart when she's away.

Maybe I'll read until the french fries are cooked. Maybe I'll keep writing.

I'm forgetting something—a supplement, vitamins, a pill. My allergies were so bad that I oscillated between cloudiness and clarity—even enjoying the torrid weather.

Something I haven't seen in a long time: a fish tank in a waiting room. Live rock, cloudy-eyed wrasse, sliver-blue chromis, a parrot fish in its mucus cocoon. Waiting for what? The tableau always looked better than the tableau.

Valley Fever's been cropping up.

Maybe I can get us a fish tank for the lighthouse or for the trailer if we stay.

East Glenn, September 21

List of possible things I want to remember: blue wasps,

dusty green plants, dark shade, warm watercolor sunsets—
things I could count on every night—a well-stocked grocery
store, a field of London rocket made from glass, a street
dead-ending in the open desert, a mesquite valley in moon-
light, summer pavement waves coming off creosote, lawn
chairs stuck in the branches of a piñon tree, light sweeping
over the small circular basin below, the brush and cacti like
coral reef at dusk or dawn.

Same Hues, September 24

I was mad that afternoon. I got the feeling I'd lost something.

I really hate that feeling, and I knew it was packed because I packed it.

Days before we started packing, I'd sketched out a few
possible lists and made diagrams conceptualizing ways to
organize what we needed to bring. I was the one who packed
it and now I don't remember where exactly I packed it because I tried packing it in a couple of different compart-
ments in a couple of different bags so I could find the best
place to keep it safe for the trip and so the space afforded
by the few bags could be used in the best possible way.

It made me wonder. Maybe I'd lost other things
too.

B said to say misplaced and not lost.

She said, Don't let it ruin the day. Then she said, This
isn't helping.

We had to take a flight immediately, so we did.

We flew quietly. Each of us was quiet. I think we were
in good enough moods, just quiet. There was some noise

obviously, but in my head, picturing the flight, there wasn't a single sound.

Or less a quiet than a feeling of the sound having been sucked out.

It got earlier as we got closer, and when we got here that's when I started worrying about losing things. I looked through every bag. I couldn't believe I was already wasting all the time we gained flying West.

I keep messing up the name of the farm where we're staying. There are three words in the name and each makes sense in relation to each of the other words in the name in any order, so that you wouldn't notice if they'd been shuffled around. Also, it makes it a little harder that here there's a place named for each of those combinations of order of the three words.

But after a while, I learn to drink hot chocolate in the heat and like it, which I hadn't done in a while and didn't think was possible.

I do some reorganizing—the plans, the permits, the contracts. Hung up the sketch of our lighthouse.

I feel uncomfortable and easy to take advantage of—I wanted to step hidden like a pink pelican into mountain shade.

It was the light meter, I thought I lost the light meter.

It's an important light meter. It's approved by the authorities that needed to approve it, something to do with space and astronomical observation here.

The light meter is calibrated to some set of specifications to measure the lux of the lighthouse as accurately as possible to make sure the light the lighthouse emits won't be bright enough to interfere with any of the astronomical studies.

These authorities also require that our light be angled downward at all times. I'm starting to think that defeats the purpose. I didn't drop what I lost. I misplaced it.

NEBRASKA

He loved her even though she was always doing something not *allll* the way right, as he put it, and with him never giving her the time. Time enough before he could say, Know what I mean?

Not all the way right like nothing wrong but nothing that made it easier.

And she loved him back even though he wasn't ever right himself and tended towards difficulty.

Things became: what's the matter?

They thought about these things, each to their own respective selves, quiet in a truck stop motel in Nevada. How they loved each other and the sound of each other breathing in a room they'll probably never be in again.

No, wait, maybe it wasn't Nevada. He had never been to

Nevada, he'll say later on when recalling this to her. It was Nebraska. They were in between.

And she'd say, Nope. Nah uh. They'd never been to Nebraska.

They held each other tightly on their way, stopped off in the middle for now. Somebody out there knows the place.

Getting there.

He could picture her in the different angles of light, of where they had been before and she was imagining the things he used to do, and how he'd do them again one day, if he could just remember himself well enough to keep trying.

WITH HIS DOG BY THE FIRE

He needs to participate in the people-way of the town, the town life when he enters.

He has to drive around Ham Woods because that's part of what he has to do. He has errands, same as everyone else—eggs, milk, bread, bananas. Things to put into other things so they have a place.

He sits down at the end of the day with his dog by the fire. But you know what comes embroidered onto the end of the day? Another day. He'll wash it down with a beer.

He smells the dust. The extra-filtered desert light through the dirty window is pinning the dust down, cooking it in.

Light stripes the floor in straight-bladed waves with the window open and the wind passing through.

He goes to check on the failed aquarium stuck outside to collect rainwater. It is coming back to life, with little dragonfly babies flick-pinching and twisting around. They've got a different name here—these things pickling in the muck—some floating in translucent balls like cocktail onions.

He'd like to phone that kid he knew from that one city who looks for the luck in things all day long. The clover kid.

At his desk again, writing long-hand he messes up and the *w* slips roundly into an *o*.

Then back to the fire with his big dog in his lap, so he doesn't have to feel like he went nowhere or got stuck.

A WATERLESS, WHITE SAND BEACH, UNDERNEATH A LOW, PURPLE SKY, PERFECTLY STILL

A moth, backlit by the blueish streetlight coming in, looks like it's swimming across the window, against and along the glass on the outside looking in at him. He feels like a fish in an aquarium. He shuts off the light and tucks himself into bed like a fish that lives in anemone.

~~~

He wants a nice glass of ice water. Two cold diamonds not quite clinking in his favorite cup, the one the B took from his work when she stopped to have lunch with him. Maybe the ice clunks in this cup, *clunking*, the more accurate word.

He saves any coupon he gets, feels guilty if he doesn't— right now he knows he has four coupons for a loaf of some
~~~

kind of bread he never buys pressed behind magnets on the fridge. It's a way to dog-ear the days like checkpoints, between when he first gets the coupon, and when he can use it or when the coupon expires. He likes to do his errands on his walks home. But pretty often, he forgets to take them off—he'll be worrying about other things like if he blew the candle out, or if he has his keys, or if the Jacques looks content enough with his bone to be alone for a short while. It's only when he's in line that he realizes he forgot.

He'd go home with two somethings, then stare at the buy-one-get-one coupon magnetted to the fridge with a performative and overly dramatic expression.

~~~

B and Jacques are still out on a walk somewhere. Where'd you go? he'll ask when they're back, and he may or may not be a little jealous. Enough to know if he wished he went with them when B asked if he wanted to go. He'd thought, Go or stay back? Stay back so he could work on his big project. Because he still has his big project to get to. Sitting at his desk weighing the options. And now they've returned and he tells them that he's actually going to go out for a walk.

~~~

You only remember the beginning of things, he'd told B once.

He thinks about how this is true of himself too. The middles always muddy. Ends, too, how one reduces itself to a detail or two. Is this part of what B was always talking about— semantic memory? Or was it the opposite, he thinks.

Arbitrary as an emotion paired with an object that lacks the ability to reciprocate that feeling—or instead an object that dials in that feeling perfectly.

Missing his favorite pinkish shirt from when he was younger, for example. If he can find it, he'll wear it for B as he serves her noodles. Elbow patches from the same material doubled up. She'll love it, he thinks. After he's changed and garnishes their plates with—he figured it out—wood sorrel, to make up for last time.

When he hands her her plate, B says she loves that color orange on him. He had no idea. Sits, looks down at his shirt. He thought it was pink. But better since she likes orange so much.

~~~

Good daily decisions to be proud of and simultaneously worried over. Like he is glad he lit the candle, but did he blow it out before leaving? Did he wear the right shoes for the weather?

The embarrassment of all he can't cross off. Because once they were with people and they had to turn back around to check if he remembered.

The certainty and dexterity of excuses he can use to convince himself otherwise is wearing out.

~~~

He burns his hand like he burned that sauce not too long ago and yells some made-up sounding word—he was trying to recall an old familial expression inside the moment he burned his hand, felt the pain and automatically needed to express that pain. But it was like things got knotted up all moving towards the same thing at the same time.

It's more that he'd burned certain fingers instead of his whole hand. His three middle fingers. Decides to use the regular lotion even though the B's been liking aloe recently and keeps recommending it.

That reminds him: Where did they put the flower that fell off the plant?

He hopes they didn't throw it out.

Where to start with an original idea as the case in point? Like do it because you love it however you can?

He thinks about a single coral planula sticking and reifying.

He imagines being where he wanted to be with B. And he tried to picture where she'd want to be—her favorite beach probably.

~~~

An echo-y, empty place where they could spend a year.

Somewhere by a handful of hills so it sounds like a cove.

A waterless, white sand beach underneath a low, purple sky, perfectly still.

B once told him how, growing up, they'd drive home at night along the soybean fields wrapping around the road. She thought she could see waves and seafoam and that the red blinking lights in the middle of the fields were lighthouses or buoy markers depending on how high up they looked.

~~~

The excuse is that the day's already closing in. Like a riddle:

What never coming is always getting closer?

As a kid he couldn't believe that John Denver was singing on the radio about how he died before he did.

He felt it was suspicious.

~~~

Worried about ending up with a single chair in a square room directly squared up with a TV five to seven feet back.

True love in a movie or book.

Sitting underneath a statue in some shade.

One of the hardest things he'd ever had to do was listen to someone reflect on the past.

These were a couple of restless days.

He needs to reel himself back in. Get control again, don't let his thoughts slip too much.

Some days he didn't feel like there was any time left.

~~~

Some days he stays up late without meaning to, into the opaque, half-lit dawn.

He thinks: Imagine how many people have done that before. And he thinks of dawn as a great word in both how it looks, letter-wise, and how it looks when he's awake for it, which is also what the word means really, that clean early morning that's more high definition than everything else.

Something like a euphoria felt in it sometimes and how the day ahead of that will feel, like a mistiness, a heavy-humid fatigue.

Let him have a look, he thinks. Talking to himself like it's a secret.

~~~

He loves seeing a pretty bird on a branch. A new place turning to an old place in his head. The feeling from seeing the bird leave the branch to seek relief in a puddle underneath an evergreen.

This made him think he might finally be rounding this bend and opening up to anything that might make him feel better without trying to figure out how to capitalize on the thing.

One blink at a time, it's important to remember.
~~~

NOT ME, JERRY-JEFF, OR MY FAMILY

What are simple actions of daily life here?

What's the normal thing to do?

I think of looking busy and looking neighborly.

I think of the Deacon, when I see him when he doesn't see. Shallowly polite, but it looks good. Most people seem to take well to it.

Most people, but not me or Jerry-Jeff or any of my family.

SPEAK

He talks. He knows this because when he talks the dog tilts its head. In the past, he'd been uncertain.

One time he recorded himself speaking to the dog so he could listen to the recording for concrete proof, but the experiment lacked validity—he could not be the control sample and the experimental sample.

When he was younger, he thought about his life a lot. Like how long it would be and where he would live and what he would do. He stopped thinking about his life a lot when he got a dog and decided that he always wanted to live somewhere sleepy.

Now he thinks about his dog being loyal and having a salt and pepper coat.

Just to be safe he thinks he will take a photograph of his dog to make sure: If it's true that his dog has a salt and pepper coat. He will take one photograph in color and another photograph in black and white and will get the photographs professionally printed 36" x 48" at 300dpi for accuracy. Then he will take a color photograph of the professionally printed black and white print of the dog with a salt and pepper coat as well as a black and white photograph of the professionally printed color print of the dog with a salt and pepper coat. He will get those photographs professionally printed 36"x 48"at 300dpi for accuracy, also.

This way both of the sets of photographs of the dog with a salt and pepper coat will take turns being the experiment sample and the control sample. He will not make a big deal about it or even think about it for too long. He just needs to be able to see it.

CLOSE ENOUGH ALWAYS

Things he can't believe in.

Things he might believe in.

Fizzy water consistency. The bubbles in his cup always go up. Seven orange cats climbing a mesquite in Tucson like a beanstalk.

Look at the good-looker leaning on a cow fence there on the Oklahoma/Texas line.

Minutiae of the mostly bumpy roads heading home. A ten month to-and-from and he can't even believe it.

Cows staring at a bush under the silver weathervane in the forever heatwave.

At least a year since he met a dog named Nibby in Truth or Consequences. He'd been on the way and looking. Traveling west is going backwards, he'd thought then, and since he'd covered some ground he should be a little younger. He pulled into a space in front of a motel's office. News on the radio: *Elderly man survives on Coca Cola for five days after fall.*

Wow, had to be the twenty-second to the twenty-sixth. Around that. In September.

Dune eyes with a crossed walk when he got out for a rest. A long day.

Now, very literal, high contrast dreams of mesquite, the same handful on repeat for weeks.

And an oceanless beach.

He let water drip onto his works when he'd gotten up to stretch. He looked down and panicked.

His work. A cult-like devotion to it.

He turned around to leave, to go and start the work over. He realized he wasn't working, he was swimming. In the green tea water of a D-shaped Lake.

Too ambiguous to understand and judge the liability of the situation without gathering any facts.

But close enough always, right?—it's a good place to land.

An empty space with a very specific and holy shape.

Something confirmed. See.

He'd been in the wrong place the whole time, listening to someone in the next room figuring it out. What they said was that it's been in the water the whole time and it's only now finally affecting us.

HE'D SAY THIS WINKING

The neighbor introduced himself to B one day when she was walking the dog. He introduced himself by saying that he hates deer and calls his wife the Secretary of War and he still fucks her.

B told me this and that when she told him her name, he said, That's an odd name. I don't know if I like it.

I'm imagining what if I talked to the neighbor because we've never talked before, and he talks like he's talking to himself, so I don't even get the chance to introduce myself.

The trees pitch in the sky over his head and the wind near-completely steamrolls his voice.

Pines and palms.

All the loblolly.

The sound the needles make when they hit the ground

and blow over it.

I'm up in the office, picturing this, and I don't know where B is.

Elsewhere obviously.

The neighbor would then, of course, start telling me more about his deer feelings. Yup, I hate them, I do, he'd say. I hate 'em. Last week, I caught a buck stuck jumping the fence.

He'd explain to me, like he did to B, that the fence he had put up—pointy and wrought iron—can do a lot of damage to deer if and when they try to hop the fence but come up short.

He'd say, They tend to get caught in these kinds of fences, so naturally I put one up. And he'd say this winking, like, You know what I mean.

He'd go on, I was lucky to catch another one. Three this season.

The last one got snagged there next to the gate, and he'd point where. Snapped through a tendon or some ligament. Dangling there from the hind leg, bleeding out until my dog...

Got so bad, had to spray off the fence after... He'd trail off again and shhhsh me. Listen, he'd say, looking me in the eye. Do you hear that? That bird there? And I'd tilt my head up to show I was listening, vaguely hearing something squawking from the top of one of the tall, scraggly pines that run the length of our brackish street.

He'd talk about how it's a familiar craw he can't place and he hates it.

I imagine myself then, picturing eggs and nests and breeding and some other innocent thing that antagonizes him. I might remember the poisoned Northern Flicker I saw dead and stiff in the grass that that old neighbor somewhere else had killed. Underneath a tree in the same neighborhood where people argued about feeding the squirrels—whether or not it was okay to do. Notes on doors. Piles of peanuts on the sidewalk.

But I'd still be standing there, watching this neighbor talk at me and repeat all the things he'd told B, everything she'd repeated back to me.

I used to work in oil, he'd say. Retired now. Yup. Congratulations to me.

While the neighbor continues talking oil, I'd picture him bathing up to his neck in it. Black oil bubbling. I'd laugh to myself, I think, sitting next to the window above the backyard.

Outside, I notice two bucks finally meeting after a slow walk across the yard. They lock antlers in front of a half-dozen other deer that have gathered in a half-circle around them. Neither one seems to have the obvious advantage, and I watch their stalemate thinking in a Texas accent, It can't be nothing like that.

In the middle of talking the neighbor might stop and about-face and head home. Like the Secretary of War had called him home. And when the neighbor gets home and opens his front door in a hurry, the swung-open bang of the door would cause a coconut to drop from a palm tree onto his head—Xs for eyes and blue and green parakeets flying around his head—right before he disappears inside.

What I could gather from what B told me is that this neighbor seems like a guy who doesn't want to get in trouble with his wife, and maybe that's the only thing that I can understand, because who does?

Still, to this day, I've never talked with him once. But I picture it, prepare for it.

In the beginning, I tried to wave hello a couple times

when I walked by walking the dog with B. Neither of us had talked to him yet but we tried to be Texas hospitable and all that, but he just stared. After a couple times, anytime I walked the dog past his place with B, when he was sitting out by his garage, I just mean mugged him, talked shit about him to B and she'd shhhsh me.

It never accomplished anything, so I stopped.

ALWAYS DOING SECRET THINGS

Thinking he might've done something good.

Just an unshaking life underneath a window, or before a window, said differently.

In order to be some kind of good person, he brainstormed codes of conduct to stick to.

To have a fighting chance at it.

Hold the door without even looking.

Keep the mailman company for a few houses.

After several postponed hiatuses, habits he had a taste for were coming back but no one else was thrilled.

Always dammed up and convolved one step too far.

Fog and love like dust kicked up at a rodeo.

Always doing secret things.

Fucked up and unfair comparisons.

How Homeric.

Good luck scaled to fit the given. Here.

But never a real chance.

When he was onced-over people had had enough—coupled with all they could take.

Another way to assess the situation seemed important as a next direction. He'd been getting pretty petty and getting it wrong. But he wanted something that he wasn't sure he'd had in a while and couldn't remember what to call it.

He had watched the dog discover its shadow in the dining room last week—the dog jumped. And when the dog found its shadow a second time, outside, the likeness blew its mind.

HE CRIED IN HIS ROOM MULTIPLE TIMES

He knows what it means to be hopeful, like the hour you get off work and you're on your walk home.

Since he got home, he'd been lying down on the couch, drinking coffee. Some dribbled down his chin onto his shirt and down his chin and around his neck, then it haloed around his head into the pillow. Butter is also all over his yellow shirt, the smell of raw potato on his skin.

Earlier, walking home, he leaned down in the grass to flick around and find a four-leaf clover, swore he saw one, but he didn't try to pick it.

He was once completely fascinated or infatuated with the things he pulled out of his own body.

Last week, as he left work, he threw away a pile of fortune cookies and a sign that said TAKE ONE. Memo said exercise in morale, company customized positive fortunes.

Once, he did something similar before at home. He flushed it all.

And on that night he sat watching a car at the end of the street burn. It was like green-brown-gray-orange-sour-blue fog that's lifting or a mist over a reef that's walloped on a rough day.

Maybe a friend from around then had been with him. All it was was some sitting on a porch and a car burning. Was all it took. No other detail, like when he bent over to look through the little patch of clover, thanks to the single pink flower that had caught his eye.

He wanted a life like that and he might have had it.

SOCIAL QUALMS

A man on the patio of the cafe is talking in a way that seems like he is trying to reach an audience, about a phase in his life when he did push-ups every fifteen minutes no matter where he was. Anywhere, I'm telling you, he says.

He says he wanted to get buff, and keeps saying it.

He says that back then life was good. That he had no real qualms about his future.

LIFE-LIKE

He didn't have any opinions and he said to himself, got-damn I love the different tones I can take with myself.

As he drove home on the back road, he was by himself, no one in the car with him or on the road passing him the other way. He remembered the guy he worked for when he first moved there, the one who had the life-size crucifix in his backyard.

Not life-like.

No way.

Not with the way it was built. It couldn't support the weight of someone. Like it wasn't built from thick enough cuts or planks of wood or lumber.

Life-size but not a hundred percent life-like. Accurate enough for a display-grade replica, he supposed, but not for use.

In the morning it was easy to see—with blue-gray frost covering up all the golden grass in the valley on the way to get some coffee and the moon still out. A break in the tree-line because of the road.

He drove by the general store with the great deli counter and the guy who makes the sandwiches and always has something to say.

He didn't turn around, but now that he's up the hill he wished he'd gone in. He sees symbolism in people seeing or seeking symbolism in things, thinking about things he's overheard in line. Dried leaves all over the car floor everywhere like fish flakes. The way something like a hat became trash as soon as it's left somewhere public. And how things just happened or *are* because they followed what happened before or whatever just was.

I BET JESUS THOUGHT THE SAME THING

Once, in the morning, on a denailed roof, on the smooth, exposed ply board, I slid.

It was just like napping, when you dream you trip and catch yourself falling so you snap up awake.

Shirtless-Gee caught my tool belt. When I stood up we looked at each other, said sheesh with a shrug, and laughed as the remaining old shingle gravel rained into the gutters. Gee told me I could buy him a few beers at lunch and that I'd have to carry up the last three ply boards and his share of shingles

Gee was a good guy, always shirtless, and everyone made fun of his nipples.

I had to climb up a thirty-two-footer my first day roofing, fully extended, with a crooked U-bar. Thirty-two feet doesn't sound like much, but when you feel the wobbles or a little sideways slip, your knees give and you know what those thirty-two feet could do to you.

Once, at work, I'd seen a guy knock himself out with a kind of rotary drill. It kicked back when he hit a knot in the wood. Got his bell rung.

This was the summer I spent roofing. Hoofing bundles of shingles up thirty-twos most afternoons. We did a few odd jobs too—decks, basements, crawl spaces. And siding. And I liked that.

This, no, it can't really be Heaven.

WHAT IS SPRAYED ON THE FRUIT CHEST KILLED AND THROWN

Just ask anyone what's next now. They'll know you won't know.

He's been watching his sneezes rainbow get lit up misty in the window. He's got one foot up on the sill.

Uncomfortable and contemplative.

Fruits or veggies?

Is he really?

To the left of the window, there's a beautiful blown out photo of the best fight between two unknown boxers there ever was. Everyone always talked about how it went eight rounds. They said seconds before the bell too. Everyone always said what if it went nine. Imagine the history. Undisputed.

This photograph was hanging above a register the first

time he saw it, inquired about it, heard a little bit of the back story, and the guy told him he'd make him a photocopy for ten.

He was so happy he wanted to shake hands. He thought he recognized one of the fighters in who he was shaking hands with—the way the guy's arm extended, like throwing a body shot.

Sipping water. Always a sip of water when a sip of water is what's needed. Cups, jars, and mugs are in the cabinet to the right of the door. Water has to be mentioned. Having to drink it because it's necessary. He thinks, Remember when you used to think it could be anything?

Some customary glance that concludes in one's judging and confirming or denying the fact there is some kind of mechanism behind all this functioning. It looks like it.

This instills jealousy, and being uneasy with happiness probably. He's not sure. He imagines leaning neutral but all his going off on tangents.

Something seen through something translucent as one objective view of something beautiful.

Citruses like tangerines—clementines—cara cara oranges.

Once, he was told, Underpromise and overdeliver and we'll be in a good place.

SORTA SOFTLY, SWEET SPOT

The ex-boxer still goes to the gym. He's got nothing else. Works out.

Slowly and sorta softly.

He hits the heavy bag in a mirror's peripheral vision for twelve rounds.

Three minutes each, thirty seconds of rest between.

Punctuated with jump roping and being steady on the speed bag.

Doesn't know how healthy it is for his head, for him to keep coming every day. He keeps his head down and just works out.

They said he looked like a young Marciano. But that nose, they'd say. It was less flat, not as classic.

He hasn't thought about being in a bad mood, until realizing now that he's in one.

And it's familiar so it's kind of nice.

He wonders why this doesn't feel like a terrible thing—what it's like to be lucky. A problem of seeing—as well as in the regurgitation of the order of events.

Beach mouth by round eight every time. That oceanic taste.

This may come in handy.

Swimming is good.

Opens ya up, they say.

Don't yearn to hate it.

It never works at first and he doesn't have any room to get further.

He relies on memories of blowing off work to push himself through rounds eleven and twelve. Sometimes, it'd been fun.

But imagine trying that today?

He's embarrassed for himself hypothetically. Already.

Things for him to be proud of: Getting paid. It feels fucking good, man, to be this many years old.

A serious question.

A dead language.

Laminate confusion.

Slow endurance.

Hummingbirds always make him happy. Woodpeckers. And there's always a dog pacing the wall.

Gift trash in the alley. Packages stolen from porches. Bows and paper and birthday cards. The well wishes and torn cards strewn in a backwards kind of confetti, and the money collected to exchange later for the local taste.

There are bronze statues of people in the park near the gym with no discernible characteristics, sitting or standing in solitude or with other bronze statues, all staring off somewhere.

The ex-boxer catches his breath with them, watching a groundsman nurse two out of three bushes back to health. The third was already healthy, planted by happenstance in a sweet spot.

WORKING AND WATCHING WOODPECKERS WORK

He thinks everyone knows that woodpeckers' tongues internally wrap around their brains. He thinks it's nothing to know this, everybody knows this.

It prevents brain damage.

They always sound like blue jays mixed with seagulls to him, maybe that's wrong.

Seeing a woodpecker always makes him feel better. They make him feel lucky to see one.

He's at work and he's watching one.

Guy he's working with asks what he's been looking at.

Tells the guy at work, look, a woodpecker. It's either a downy woodpecker or a hairy woodpecker. I can't tell. They almost look the same but one's bigger—I forget which is which already.

The guy at work says, Where?

Right there.

That's a woodpecker? That's not what I pictured, the guy at work says. I pictured Woody the Woodpecker.

Yeah, those ones, that kind lives around here too. They live around most of the country I think, he tells the guy at work. Pileated woodpeckers. They get big, like a small hawk.

He likes this guy at work. This guy's kind of down all the time, sad. The guy's younger than him.

One day he asked the guy, Do you want my old guitar? It's missing a string, probably work fine otherwise.

HIS THOUGHTS ARE BLOODY, OR NOTHING WORTH

It wouldn't be polite to try to speak or ask for help, he thought. His mouth was full of blood—the taste of metal, and the salt from all the slush stinging.

This was a new even, you know, a new place to stand back from and to look at it all, circumstantially.

Nah, none of this, he said to himself in his head. He knows he's the only one in there, in his head, but he didn't want to let doubt win.

He was being matter-of-fact, not sarcastic or facetious.

Now he was only thinking about trying to finish his errand. If he didn't do it now he'd have to come back. Like, would it be more worth it to run in and grab what he needed—bloody-faced and risk people seeing him like that?

No. Blood all over the car door on the way back in, the

inside and outside of the driver's door window.

At home he lay down on the couch, playing dead.

He had been a paper boy, and a boxer at another point. A property manager, a slumlord.

Took a few beatings in the ring, you know. Back when sparring with the older guys, left bloody but nothing that left his head light enough.

Besides the tinker percussion of the water heater, there is the general sort of sound now, like trash blowing somewhere.

Sometimes it's just want you need—that peaceful, slow-moving whoosh. A car pulling in.

Throughout the next few weeks, for some reason or other, he keeps overhearing people talk about Hamlet.

But then he thinks, No, that's the wrong one right now. It doesn't make sense.

A POINT

He reached a point, and it's not like he was trying to get to this point, he didn't want to reach this point, at all actually, he was actively trying to avoid reaching this point, he didn't want to get to this point, it feels debilitating, even before he got here, he tried pretty hard to think of how to avoid getting to a point, getting to this point, it's something like an overarching inability, a fog, frustration, it doesn't have to do directly with work, but work is affected by it, generally, it's hard to say what this getting to a point means, now, he's trying to get at that now, to figure out what he means, what it means for him, as in can he figure out what he means to say or which way to go from here? generally he hopes to seem straightforward, he doesn't want to come off too dramatic but he gets the feeling it will seem like he is being dramatic, and if he is, fine, as long as he can see that and see why or how he got to this point, under duress of a relatively simple stretch of a strange year, he called it a wash and it is a was, but he's trying move beyond this point he's reached, so he can enjoy the everything else and be good company for others, he could say that he's trying to get to the point of getting to a point, but he keeps getting distracted, for better or for worse, he keeps thinking about and talking about woodpeckers when he shouldn't be, especially here, working, his work has had a little bit to do with them very indirectly, he talks about them often, looks for them when he's working outside, like the day after a freeze, a yellow-bellied sapsucker flew between two pines, it spent the day pecking and he kept saying, oh yeah, it's in heaven, sap runs better after a freeze, he heard this somewhere and he remembers living where taps were set up all through the woods and there was even a maple syrup tap and deli in between a couple of the towns, sapsuckers are a kind of woodpecker he thinks, different name but really they do the same thing, most importantly he appreciates them in the same way, a supsucker and a woodpecker, for the sapucker, sapsucking is what they do after woodpecking, so they, sapsuckers, for whatever reason have been named, commonly for the second thing they do instead of the first thing they do, more or less, here, he started thinking about them because he heard one and looked around for it, started thinking about them often, then started thinking about why he thinks about them often and whether he needs to justify it or not, What have I been doing? he thinks, Working, walking, sitting on the porch, laying in the sun on the floor like the dog, watching the dog lie in the sun.

COOKED WATER

Something hard pressed to be stopped.

Look, he thinks.

A train rolls by.

You actually can't see it but you can hear it. The rolling, the train whistle. Birds at home on the water taking off. While he's here cooking eggs, cleaning up, speaking softly to himself in the quiet of the dining room. Now, finally, eating his eggs with a spoon.

There's one leaf in the yard. Not his yard. It's the start of October and it's more comfortable this way.

One at a time.

He'd, from now on, spend his time only going to the slow places—a decision he was finally able to make—newly open and plain, or failing places on the way out, depleting and disappearing. He could relate to such a slow dimming.

Once he won a trip to Vegas, Atlantic City, and Reno.

In that order.

This was right before he took a job in Toledo.

In Toledo, he had a good job. The best good job he ever had. Two-digit number hourly wage. He'd go around checking up on abandoned homes that a property management company owned and had to keep empty or clean out or make sure were still trashed and unlivable. Three houses, or so, every trip up was what the company wanted.

The houses were all bigger than any house he'd lived in. And here, empty and abandoned. Almost a whole town of it.

When he wasn't on one of these incremental trips, he sat in an office loading up pictures of the properties onto a computer. Proof of vacancy. When the pictures were on the computer, the company knew.

One property in Toledo had a shed with a dead dog in it. On the side of it facing the house was painted: *Stacey's kids suck dick.*

Something had happened. He had a look and left. He didn't want to take a picture of that.

Eventually the company collapsed and that was it for him, half glad. He'd made some money. That was that till it was gone.

If he could go back though.

Except, Back from when? To where?

He wanted to clarify a point he'd made. He could embellish and have that. Remind himself he had to at least work a little for it.

Then what? If he were able to iron out the information, a stiff and loose understanding?

A practice course in impulse—is that *feeling it out?*

He would have to have to lay down the law. Stop it

from going on and on. Asked a neighbor once if they were level, then he leveled out the wrinkles like it was a blanket and he was just making the bed.

And what that says about him. Broken dishes in the sideboard downstairs.

Lucky he got himself up long enough to go anywhere. It's being like this that certainly does exacerbate things. How he can't leave things be and what that says about him in a situation.

Like something convenient, collapsible, and storable.

Boiled over.

And after, whatever was left in the pan was his life. It had an electrical taste to it when he tried to have a sip.

On one visit, when he was finally alone, you shoulda seen what he did.

He used to get phone calls about dream vacations.

Have a ring at it.

Win a trip with, if you do it right, only some stipulations.

He could name all the kinds of fish he'd want to see swimming on the reef: slippery dick and other wrasse, a queen triggerfish, cuttlefish, stoplight parrotfish, spotted cowfish, lionfish, grouper, snapper, flounder, sergeant major, tangs, angels.

THERE HE IS

I tried to fish. I felt like fishing that day. I wanted to go through the motions of it. Attach a lure to the end of the line, cast out and reel, cast out, reel in, cast out.

About five casts in, I'm snagged, real stuck. I didn't have any patience that day.

I pull the fishing rod back as hard as I can, the line singing taut, then the lure lets go of the snag, it's flying back, stings me in the ditch of the arm.

I remember looking on the ground to see where it landed, to avoid stepping on it. And as I was looking down, I noticed it stuck in the ditch of my arm, a hook buried beyond the barb.

After struggling, yanking at it, stretching out my skin unsuccessfully, with the barb doing its job, I said to myself out loud and panicked, *Pliers, yes, pliers.* With the pair of needle-nose I pinched my skin hard, the skin right over where the barb would be, to try to pinch the barb down.

I hear or feel a crunch.

I slide the hook out, the barb all flattened.

It's funny to me. All the fishing we did as kids and something like this never happened to me or any of the cousins. Sometimes we slipped on wet rocks. Sometimes we walked out into a mussel patch by accident, without sandals or water shoes, and got cut.

After thinking about this, I walk back over to the table.

It is a too-bright day, hard to see things easily.

But I think I see an eagle above the trees some way across the lake, where the land sticks out and bends back and part of the lake is hidden.

I feel peaceful for a moment.

I hear a shout behind me.

There he is.

WHAT IS THE NATURE OF LIFE?

Sun flashed off some lamination and it was in his eyes. They had name tags and got to it right away and wanted to know what he thought.

What he thought about what? he asked the guy at the door.

The guy held open the screen door with a foot in a black shoe because his arms held tightly onto a briefcase and a lady's arm.

He could have finished his dishes by now, definitely, at least by the time this meeting of the minds finally grand finale-ed.

He had promised himself that one last swig when the dishes were done.

The guy at the door prodded, So?

He could have socked the guy in the mouth on account of the melodrama of the whole thing and how it could've gone further.

Is it okay to come back later? he said.

Bless you, the guy said.

But now, he would have to look outside, keep a lookout.

Could've, probably should've, pretended to not be home. Be at work, have a job.

When he closed the door, the sun eclipsed the doorway on the living room floor and he went back to finish washing the dishes.

THE REST OF IT

He's digging a hole. He's been digging it for a little bit now. He's out of work but his wife, B, still works. He could not dig without her. He used to work in a small restaurant in town until he could not work there anymore. Before he started digging, he used to do all of the laundry and he used to make sure the clothesline was taut and he used to work at that restaurant. He had already done enough, he thinks. People ask him,

Hey, watcha doin, bawd?

Digging, he says.

Watcha diggin' for?

Well, why don't you wait to find out.

Eh, why you diggin'?

I've done the rest of it, he says, waving his trowel.

SAME AS ANYTHING

He kicked right into the horseshoe crab and it wobbled a bit. He wobbled too and thought if it was a rock or not.

He decided to flip it over and guide it back with a stick he found.

There were layers repeating themselves in the dark being lapped at and this in front of him needed to be figured out.

It was what he had for now.

And it was the same as anything.

It all happened all clunked around like ice cubes in a drink-finished cup at the end of what felt like vacation. This was in the Carolinas at night, quiet and sore.

He said, You can, I swear.

And then, I promise.

And then, I really swear.

He watched the horseshoe crab slide into the water and away.

At the end of the beach there was a pier, most of it taped off from storm damage. Underneath the pier he took his clothes off. He felt the chilly and salty air and, for a while, he slalomed between the posts that held the pier up, looking around until he sat down at some point.

It was what was there.

Only the ocean and some blankness over it.

WHEN THE SUN IS BRIGHT

I will probably drown in my own pool, middle-aged.

If we even have a pool.

On some sunny morning.

After breakfast.

When I can't finish what you couldn't.

So we should remember to eat light from now on, and to avoid places with pools.

WALKING

I walk a lot. I like walking.

I took a walk today just to get out of the apartment. Came back with a six-pack that I didn't really need or want. Then I walked to the fridge to the living room to the bathroom to the living room, sat for a second, then walked back to the kitchen and fridge to actually get a beer, and back to the living room. One lap, maybe a repeated stop or two. There were five more after that and each one got faster.

I've got blue pants on with a single dot of pink from a bleach drop. White socks, brown shoes. I change into the black shoes whenever I leave the apartment. This is how my grandfather dressed, plus he'd stuffed his breast pocket with smokes, lottery tickets, a lighter, and a little pencil.

A kind of uniform, complete with pink bleach drops. He was a cleaner.

I think I want to get some scratch tickets next time I'm at the store. If I remember to I will.

Walking earlier, I threw a couple shadowboxed punches. Had to stop and put the six-pack down for a sec. Looked at my reflection in some storefront window. I was thinking about a move, so I made the move, because I wanted to feel myself go through the motions and see myself make those motions. Felt self-conscious that someone on the other side of the window was looking at me like I was performing for them.

This comes from the same part of my brain that allows me to talk to myself out loud in public: What should someone do when they over-squirt the appropriate amount of mustard onto the plate for the corn dog? What is their responsibility? Should the extra mustard, if clean and crumb free, be siphoned back into the mustard bottle?

It's kind of a boring place to walk here. So I have boring thoughts. There's nothing for me to connect with. Like a right hook connecting after a parry.

At the grocery store late one night, a few weeks ago, I thought I was going to have to fight someone whose name seemed like it would be Timoly. Timoly said, My bad. So I said back to Timoly, Definitely is. And Timoly called me a pussy. I was just mad because it's really not hard to be a person who goes unnoticed peacefully, but Timoly couldn't and kept cutting me off, waving around a bag of whole wheat tortillas.

After the exchange, I kept walking up the aisle towards the seltzer water, laughing, and I kept thinking, What?

What?

Imagine how dumb that would've been.

Good to be safe walking around. Bundle up, hide most of your face. Hat and shades.

Floating right through.

The grass will be greener there once I make it through. If this could hurry up and be over with.

Go there or go back.

I was walking up Main Street, with these sharp sneezes going on.

Remembered getting my nose cauterized a dozen or more times. I'd be covered in my own blood after two or three rounds. Wipe it from my face and wipe it on my shirt with my red glove. Could never tell how much there was till after, cooling off and finding form in the mirror.

I remember being covered in flour, breathing it in, sneezing, after dumping the fifty pound bag into the dough machine. Don't turn it on yet. Step back for a sec, let it settle, that thing will take your arm off, repeating in my head all these years later.

Fishing, it's the same feeling as getting caught with the hook in the crook of my arm, trying to get it unstuck from the weeds.

I want to want nothing.

I want to take a nap. But I never do.

Do you think it will turn out?

Is this real or not? Frame it. Hang it up. Please tell me what this is.

What was I doing?

I'm trying to engage with myself.

Walking. Talking. Thinking.

Today I did wake up. I got out of bed and put the uniform on.

Being good this month but also not quite as good as I can be.

I like to keep walking once I start. Take a few laps.

I've been adding some paprika to my breakfast. I keep forgetting to get a thing of Cavender's and a lemon. I'm not sure if I like Cavender's, but it's been a while, and it would be something to do to get some and try it again.

Cavender's and scratch tickets.

(THANKS FOR COMING) IN AT ALL

The people around here.

Maybe it was him. New here, probably why.

New to them, too, who've been here and he probably hadn't picked up on something.

Who knows. He sure doesn't.

Only two hours away from somewhere else he'd lived but he'd never seen a thing like it in his life.

People don't listen, then repeat back all the wrong things in some other order and in a tone.

Then who gets confronted or pushed around?

He does.

Boss says, You know what I heard?

And he shakes his head at Boss without looking.

And boss tells him.

He's tries to think how, at the end of every day, he could do something for someone, some way to be nice.

He doesn't see anyone or know anyone anymore. They don't say good morning to each other at work. Boss talks, then there's work, and home again.

He goes to head to the store on the way home sometimes, and thinks, I can hold the door for someone. Then at the front of the store he remembers that the doors are automatic.

How could he forget? He goes to the store almost every day.

Anyways.

It's another thing.

In the morning he'll punch in.

And when he's clocked the right numbers in, the machine will confirm: IN AT All.

I TOOK MY BABY DOWN TO BROWN'S LOBSTER POUND

I owed my baby one. She'd said she always wanted to go. These were two different things. Me owing her and us going. In a way. I owed her one and had the answer because I thought of it. Brown's Lobster Pound. Perfect surprise because I needed to show some sort of gesture right then. Two parts sorry, one part celebration. Her saying she always wanted to go was a different matter. For a while, she'd said she always wanted to go. But I think she forgot about it, or the idea of going. I knew she'd like it. That was obvious. It's her kind of place. I didn't forget because I had actually been. She hadn't. She had at one point talked about it all the time, how I never took her but just talked the place up so much. I'd gone a few times growing up. Best lobster rolls. Everything straightforward. I remember getting steamers there in a big basket as a kid. You'd love it, I told her. She loves steamers and she didn't grow up with them. I know a lot of people who didn't grow up eating them and don't like them when they try them.

My baby wanted to go. My baby's name is Buggy and so I call her that. I can't repeat what she calls me. Buggy'll be my wife one day. To be safe, I've got to establish and reestablish, in her eyes, that I can handle that kind of business. Be as provisional as necessary, and that's tough, and even go beyond that. We talk about it a lot. I've been told many, many things that are better to be remembered than forgotten, which, of course, has happened. When we first got together, I told her about the lobster rolls at Brown's, how it was a short drive even though it was only a state away. She's from a whole handful of those big states that take a few days to drive through. Half the country. Sometimes I'll ask, But if you had to pick one to be from? Buggy's always got Amarillo on the mind. I love that about her. And so Brown's was kind of regionally exotic to her. Quite the opposite of what she grew up with and in some ways exactly the same. Odd that we hadn't gone. I wasn't trying to keep her from it or it from her. Kind of felt like sometimes I didn't even know if I remembered Brown's the right way. Am I sure it's Brown's where I was thinking of? I looked up pictures and was almost certain it was. We just never took the trip. There were times it just didn't come up for a while. When it did we talked about regional delicacies. My steamers, roast beef, fried clam rolls, baked haddock. Her Jell-O salads, mostly. You have to say something like green-leaf salad if you want a classic lettuce-based garden salad, otherwise they give you all kinds and colors of Jell-O. She also had buckets of ranch at the state fair. I'd tease her frequently about going. I'd say, Let's go get one of those famous rolls, and really we'd go to the grocery store, get an imitation-seafood roll on the way home at one of the circle-store spots that speckle that mini-region. The stores right in the middle of a rotary. Otherwise, we'd get sidetracked.

Brown's is out on the side of this little salt marsh. The water, the marsh grass and sandbars. Blue, green, and gold. I could picture her sitting, sweating beautifully and happily there in the humid sun on the porch of this little seafood cafeteria. On the other side of a little poor man's Cape Cod looking town. Bars, restaurants, stores for novelty T-shirts and beach miscellany, tattoo parlors. Brown's was a couple miles beyond all this, right off the main road. Kind of out there but there's space around it because of that, the ocean and marsh, a big sun-faded, salt-rusted billboard across the street advertising fireworks.

I wanted it to be a big surprise. I set it up that way. I tried to be sneaky. I wanted to surprise her. I wanted her to be surprised and this would be the hardest to successfully pull off. And I owed her. So we went to Brown's Lobster Pound.

For some time before this I'd been acting despicably. I was working through a sort of comparatively logical posture toward the things of my life. At work, to colleagues, to strangers. Buggy told me this. She declared me non compos mentis and I asked how. I was letting a lot of things slip, she said. Eschewing all responsibility. I only made poor decisions and even poorer excuses regarding my decisions. I wasn't even trying. I had nothing to do and I pretended that whatever it was I was doing was extremely important. Critical. It was an act.

Brown's would be the remedy. I'd be off the hook. She would like the drive, too, through little tourist towns on the ocean between Mass and New Hampshire. I love the drive.

I'm always interested in the growing frequency of Live Free or Die license plates. I told her about a couple errands I wanted to do. I had it figured out. I asked if she wanted to come with me. I said I was thinking maybe heading out early afternoon, not too bad, it's the middle of the week. Because we always like to go out when it's slow. I threw in that we could think of something else to do after.

She said yeah and asked where we were going, because if we were going to be near the big nice health-food store she wanted to get a couple things to try. So when we left I think she thought, Errands. At any point after maybe twenty minutes of driving I knew she'd ask where we were going because of this health food store request. And Buggy did. She asked how the big nice health food store was going to figure in, if this was the direction we were heading. I always think I'm good at making a surprise for someone. But then I just end up telling the person what the surprise is early because I get too excited. It feels good to think of a really good surprise, a little treat. I thought Brown's would be a real treat because Buggy's become such a seafood freak. And we could still do a couple errands after. I tried not to say anything. Brown's Lobster Pound. I kept thinking to myself not to say anything, let the surprise be a surprise.

She made a few guesses. She didn't get it though.

Are we going to see somebody?

No.

Ice cream?

There's plenty of closer places.

But there's that new one I heard about. It's this way, I think. Is that where?

Nope.

Hmm, some kind of big thing to look at? I don't know.

...

She got mad when she thought we were going to get another dog, because I laughed. I started listing off possible names. In the back of my mind I was still half-worried she wouldn't remember Brown's. But ultimately it didn't matter. I was getting points, I hoped, for taking her to a delicious and classic place. I kept changing the radio song and Buggy got pissed. She said, Stop changing the stations but I didn't and she wouldn't talk to me. I'd let myself get sucked into the argument, forgetting my goal. It started us both feeling slightly sour. So I sang her a song from my Catholic school days called "God Is the Gas in My Go-Cart" and did the accompanying dance motions with my right hand while driving with my left. The last line is "Filled up with God, I can't fail." It was good. That was the song we all loved singing when we had to be singing something. Some assembly or spring show. My song turned it all around and I felt briefly but densely confident I pulled it off. It was almost… bad. So I was excited that our moods re-lightened. And obviously I was excited we were going to Brown's Lobster Pound. It's not like I wasn't going there to not eat.

We passed the handful of suburban exits, stands of trees, exits, trees, salt marshes, blank spaces, parking lots, firework stands, beach towns. I took an exit and woods turned to beach to marsh to beach lined with RV parking. Then there's the permanent slow crawl through the center of town, all due to the high concentration of groups of people in flip-flops, carrying coolers, dragging carts and wagons, beach chairs, pails, kids, and boogie boards. The town turned to parking, back to beach, then a long empty stretch of salt marsh. When we made it through, I elbowed Buggy. I could see the Brown's sign. I pointed.

Buggy yelled, Oh!

I remember thinking, I fucking pulled it off.

I said, Hell yeah, baby.

We parked next to a yellow car with orange-and-red flame graphics on the back window. It wasn't raining but I smelled or was reminded of the smell of hot and wet concrete. Standing up out of the car, in the tarseal parking lot, I pictured it steaming off in the sun, the mist turning to the little waves of heat distortion.

We wrapped around the pastel yellow and beige-brown building. I didn't remember which counter was for which. This is when I start to get really anxious. Situations like this, the etiquette and flow of a place. I was certain I'd been to Brown's before. I kept thinking, This is the place, yeah, this is the place. We stood in line outside, at the first counter, bickering about which counter to order from. We ordered from that first counter and it worked. We got lobster rolls and BLTs and a big root beer. I looked for real beer and didn't see it. And we didn't really know what next or where to pick up the food or listen for it. We had a number on a torn corner of paper. We went inside and stood around at the lobster tanks waiting. The tanks were in a room just inside the screen door near the indoor counter. Buggy wanted to look at the lobsters and I wanted to see if you just had to buy the beer inside. But then I saw on a sign it was a BYOB only place, and also up near the ceiling along the whole restaurant, shelves of beer. This almost got me too. I sweated over this in the bad way. Cooly. I wanted to drink beer there because I knew I could. I didn't have beer. They didn't sell it. I had to walk it off. Walked around the place to get a lay of the land. It's deceiving from the outside. It feels so big in there. The wood's much darker inside, not being sun-bleached. A long cement floor. Picnic-style tables, worn soft and splintery like driftwood. There were other salt-hued and faded things. It was really a pretty place.

Back in front of the lobster tanks I said, You're On Camera Smile, in an announcer-like voice, a voice of announcement and warning, like at the airport, pointing to a sign. Buggy thought the lobsters in their tank were so cute. I think we're about to eat one, I said.

We sat at a table near a lady with an intercom microphone calling out numbers. We sat down looking at the little torn paper every time to check if it was our number. I sat there sweating, looking at the shelves of empties lining the ceiling. Beers from all over the world. Beers that came to be drunk here with lobster or steamers or a fried-seafood plate. *Seven-ninety-eight-B.* We took our food from a counter inside that neither of us noticed until our number was called. First we went up to the counter inside we initially noticed, then we were pointed to where we needed to go. We took our food on two orange trays and walked the length of the place and outside. Me and my baby sat around back on a tiled-top picnic bench at the edge of the deck. We sat above the marsh, looked over the water and grass as we ate. We talked about planting strawberries and eating popcorn at the pier back home. She told me she couldn't believe I'd never noticed that about the guy who's always at the bar. I never really caught it. We looked across the water. I tried to see something in the water. A fin, a wake, a fish jumping, a boat, a seagull.

I was listening to Buggy and then I thought about how I tend to talk a lot when we go out, because I only really talk to her. And that's fine. It's not even the same kind of communication.

I said, It's funny to think how do we be happy now? Like what next? When we're done eating and just drive home.

Buggy said, I'm happy now.

And now I keep thinking about this other thing from the week after all this. I was happy. I don't think they're connected. Buggy went to the ER for stomach pain, everything was fine, she said I could say this. And after, at home, Buggy made me stay in a different room all night because I'd been on a very noticeable few-days-long streak of being funny and making her laugh and it hurt when she laughed.

BUT IT COULD'VE BEEN ANYWHERE

One of those big picnic bench swings. I don't remember who I knew that would've had one in their yard, only that someone was always yelling at us to be careful.

Just the other day I spit out a real-sugar version of grocery store brand Dr. Pepper. There are probably thousands of things or more that also taste like dust that aren't. I got a mouthful of it more than a few times.

The mail comes every single day and I look forward to it. Except Sundays. I slide it out against the grit that somehow gets inside the mailbox. The wind, I bet. But I picture the mailperson sprinkling it in.

We'd called it supper because dinner sounded too formal.

We all got good tips that week.

thinking, Does anyone feel this way at all?

I've walked on or under three natural bridges in the past five years.

Fish tanks, parakeets, sunflower seeds.

Vaseline and bacitracin.

Got a hook caught in the ditch of my arm once trying to get B.'s line unstuck from the brush. I had to use pliers to crunch the barb in my skin down flat so I could slide it out.

Strawberry-shaped hummingbird feeder. Halfmoon lake.

Pork chops and applesauce. PuPu Platters close to or in December, I guess. Whenever we went into town.

Over the years, there were several attempts to repurpose the "TV room" but it was always called just that.

Maybe I'll move into the old house one day. Blueberries at the lake, strawberries in the backyard, trundle beds in the garage. Threw the last cast out and caught a good ol' largemouth bass.

A single unworn edge on the piece of green sea glass.

Weather here like this reminds me of weather there like that and getting in arguments. Pushing X's into bug bites with dirt-clod fingernails.

There's always a place I don't want to leave.

I don't know if C died or not but sometimes I try to find out.

Now twenty to thirty minutes into the woods minimum for a walk with the dog.

Back in Tucson near Doolen Fruitvale: Stacey Toole on a sign heading west.

The sun on the floor in the kitchen. The dog in the sun. Saddle up.

<u>THANK YOU</u>

Thank you Raegan for helping me get all these stories off
the floor. Thank you Mom and Dad for all your love and
help. Thank you Diane Williams, Liza St. James, Madelaine
Lucas, and Zach Davidson for all the help through the
years, for publishing my work at NOON, and for being
the first ones to publish my work at all. Thank you Jordan
Castro for editing and publishing some of my early work
at Tyrant & thank you for all the other ways you've helped
me out, always grateful. Thank you Harris Lahti for all
your help, too, with this book, with a handful of stories,
for letting my throw ideas at you. Thank you Jon Lindsey
for starting Cash 4 Gold and including me. Thank you
Evan Lavender-Smith, Robert Lopez, Babak Lakghomi,
Jake Lenderman, Nicolette Polek, Kathryn Scanlan, and
Merve Emre for your blurbs, kind words, for reading

ACKNOWLEDGMENTS

These stories first appear, sometimes in a slightly different form, in NOON Annual: "Bud," "Daily," "It'd Be Nice to Have a Sharp-Looking Cooler," "Personally," "I Am a Little World," "A Life in a Small House," "It's Come to This," "Mysteries of the West," "With His Dog by the Fire," "Not Me, Jerry-Jeff, or My Family," "He Cried in His Room Multiple Times," "I Bet Jesus Thought the Same Thing," "His Thoughts Are Bloody, or Nothing Worth," "There He Is," "What Is the Nature of Life?," "The Rest of It," "I Took My Baby Down to Brown's Lobster Pound"; in New York Tyrant: "The Champ is Here," "Woodpecker," "Craigs and Gregs," "Social Qualms," "Same as Anything," "(Thanks for Coming) in at All"; in The Baffler: "A Year in the Face"; in Fence: "Licking the Spoon," "He'd Say This Winking," "Cooked Water"; in Hotel: "Nebraska," "A Waterless, White Sand Beach, Underneath a Low, Purple Sky, Perfectly Still," "What Is Sprayed on the Fruit Chest, Killed and Thrown"; in Muumuu House: "Speaking Candidly," " Juice," "Pet Fences"; in Joyland; "Grocery Stores Have Different Names, Regionally," "Paw," "Speak," "But It Could've Been Anywhere"; in Post Road: "Display," "The Ladder," "Walking"; in Sleepingfish: "Magnesium Dreams"; in The Collagist (or The Rupture): "Whatever It Is," Life-Like"; in Columbia Journal: " Close Enough Always," "Always Doing Secret Things," "Sorta Solftly, Sweet Spot"; in Annulet Poetics: "A Point"; in Neutral Spaces: "When the Sun Is Bright"; in The Quarterless Review: "Working and Watching Woodpeckers Work."